Disney · PIXAR

RATATOUILLE
(rat·a·too·ee)

MENU

Written by
Victoria Saxon

Illustrated by
Scott Tilley & Jean-Paul Orpiñas

Designed by
Tony Fejeran

Inspired by the art and character
designs created by Pixar

A GOLDEN BOOK · NEW YORK

Copyright © 2007 Disney Enterprises, Inc./Pixar. All rights reserved. Published in the United States
by Golden Books, an imprint of Random House Children's Books, a division of Random House, Inc., New York,
and in Canada by Random House of Canada Limited, Toronto, in conjunction with Disney Enterprises, Inc.
Golden Books, A Golden Book, A Little Golden Book, the G colophon, and the distinctive
gold spine are registered trademarks of Random House, Inc.

Library of Congress Control Number: 2006937776

ISBN: 978-0-7364-2423-3

www.goldenbooks.com

www.randomhouse.com/kids/disney

Printed in the United States of America

10 9 8 7 6 5 4 3 2 1

This is
the story
of Remy,
a little rat
with

BIG

dreams.

Remy wasn't like all the other rats. For one thing, he had an extraordinary sense of

SMELL.

He also had a taste for finer food.

And *THAT* is why Remy dreamed of being . . .
a *CHEF!*

But Django,
Remy's father,
had another
job for him . . .

. . . poison checker. The compost heap was where the rats got all their food. Remy had the important job of sorting the safe garbage from the bad garbage. This was NOT part of his dream.

One day,
the rats had to flee
their home. A HUMAN
had discovered them!
As the human chased them,
the rats ran to their
ESCAPE boats and
floated into
the sewers.

Remy got separated from the others
and ended up near a fancy French
restaurant—in
PARIS.

The restaurant used to belong to Remy's idol, the late and great chef, Auguste Gusteau. Now Gusteau popped up in Remy's

IMAGINATION.

Then—whoops!

Remy fell from
the skylight into
the kitchen.

The restaurant
was an EXCITING place
for Remy, but it was
SCARY, too.

In the kitchen, Remy cooked a pot of soup to replace what the garbage boy had spilled. The garbage boy was named Linguini. After that, Linguini and Remy became friends. *AND* they were a secret cooking team.

SHHHH!

Meanwhile, Django and the rest of the
rat colony made a new home in the dark,
wet sewers under Paris. Things weren't
the same without Remy. Django
kept hoping he would
find his son one day.

But Remy was happy. He did miss his family, but he had found his place in the world. Working together, Linguini and Remy made great food, even though Remy had to stay hidden. The human chefs did not want a rat in their kitchen!

Once, after cooking a wonderful meal, the chefs celebrated in the kitchen. Remy celebrated, too, in the back alley, where . . .

. . . he found his brother EMILE!

Emile took Remy **HOME**
to the rats' new colony
in the sewer.

Of course, Django was HAPPY to see Remy again!

But Remy didn't feel as if he belonged with the rats anymore. He didn't want to go back to smelling garbage.

"I have friends, a place to live, work that I love," Remy tried to explain to his dad. "I'll come back often," he said. But for now he had to return to his new home and the restaurant. Remy's dad didn't understand.

Remy went back to being a little chef. Meanwhile, Linguini was falling in LOVE!

Soon Linguini found out that he was the owner of the restaurant! And the restaurant was becoming very famous. Linguini enjoyed the attention.

Linguini decided he didn't need Remy anymore. They **ARGUED.**

Remy felt very
SAD
and
ALONE.

Who was his
family now?

But Linguini needed *HELP.*

He had to cook a special dinner for a special guest. And Linguini told Remy he was SORRY. UH-OH! The other chefs didn't like rats, so they left.

Django saw
Linguini being kind
to Remy.
He asked everyone
in the rat colony to
pitch in to help make
the special dinner.
All the rats became
little chefs!

With the rats' help,
the meal was a success.
The SPECIAL dish was
ratatouille!

The rats also helped Remy **CHASE** away the health inspector . . .

. . . who still **CLOSED** the restaurant for having rats.

LA RATATOUILLE

That gave Remy and his friends an idea. They opened a **NEW** one!

And Remy's colony ate at the restaurant, too—enjoying all the fine food they could ever want.

Menu

Best of all,
Remy became
a chef at last.

"I am **PROUD** of you
no matter what,"
Django said.